I SPY EASTER BOOK FOR KIDS AGES 2-5

A CUTE & INTERACTIVE PICTURE BOOK, FUN EASTER ACTIVITY BOOK WITH GUESSING GAMES FOR PRESCHOOLERS AND TODDLERS | PERFECT GIFT AND EASTER BASKET STUFFER FOR BOYS AND GIRLS

This book belongs to:

....

....

....

I SPY WITH MY LITTLE EYE SOMETHING BEGINNING WITH...

A IS FOR

APPLE

I SPY WITH MY LITTLE EYE SOMETHING BEGINNING WITH...

B IS FOR

BUNNY

I SPY WITH MY LITTLE EYE SOMETHING BEGINNING WITH...

 IS FOR

CANDLE

I SPY WITH MY LITTLE EYE SOMETHING BEGINNING WITH...

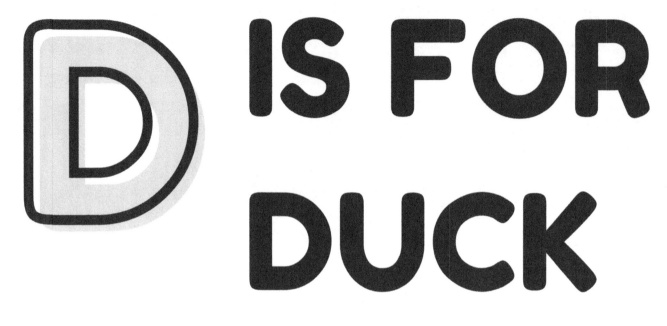

D IS FOR DUCK

I SPY WITH MY LITTLE EYE
SOMETHING BEGINNING WITH...

E IS FOR

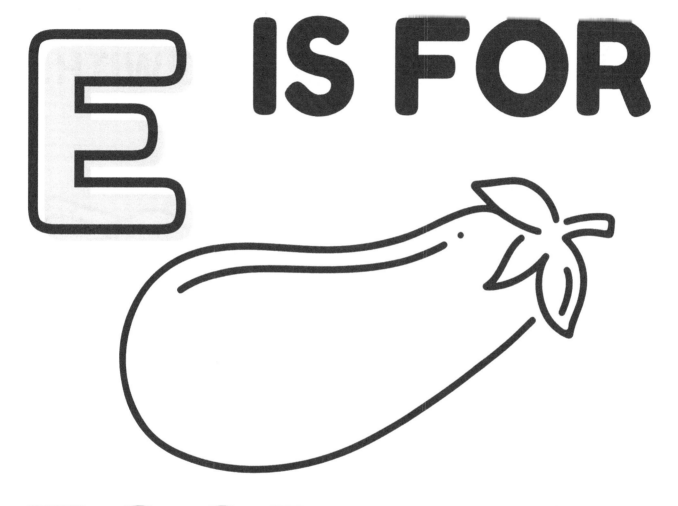

EGGPLANT

I SPY WITH MY LITTLE EYE SOMETHING BEGINNING WITH...

F IS FOR FISH

I SPY WITH MY LITTLE EYE SOMETHING BEGINNING WITH...

G

IS FOR

GOAT

I SPY WITH MY LITTLE EYE SOMETHING BEGINNING WITH...

H IS FOR

HAT

I SPY WITH MY LITTLE EYE SOMETHING BEGINNING WITH...

I IS FOR

ICE CREAM

I SPY WITH MY LITTLE EYE SOMETHING BEGINNING WITH...

J IS FOR

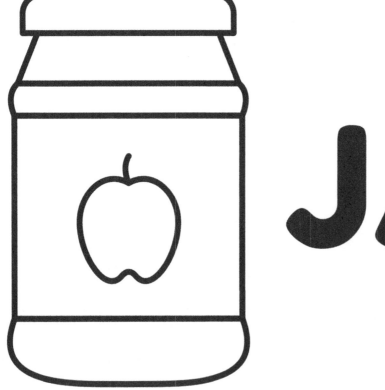

JAM

I SPY WITH MY LITTLE EYE
SOMETHING BEGINNING WITH...

K IS FOR

KING

I SPY WITH MY LITTLE EYE
SOMETHING BEGINNING WITH...

L IS FOR LILY

I SPY WITH MY LITTLE EYE SOMETHING BEGINNING WITH...

M IS FOR

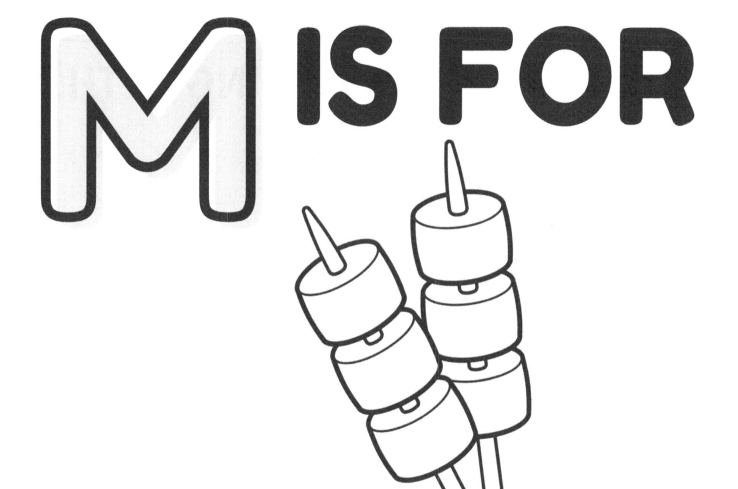

MARSHMALLOWS

I SPY WITH MY LITTLE EYE SOMETHING BEGINNING WITH...

N IS FOR

NEST

I SPY WITH MY LITTLE EYE
SOMETHING BEGINNING WITH...

IS FOR

ONION

I SPY WITH MY LITTLE EYE
SOMETHING BEGINNING WITH...

P IS FOR PLANT

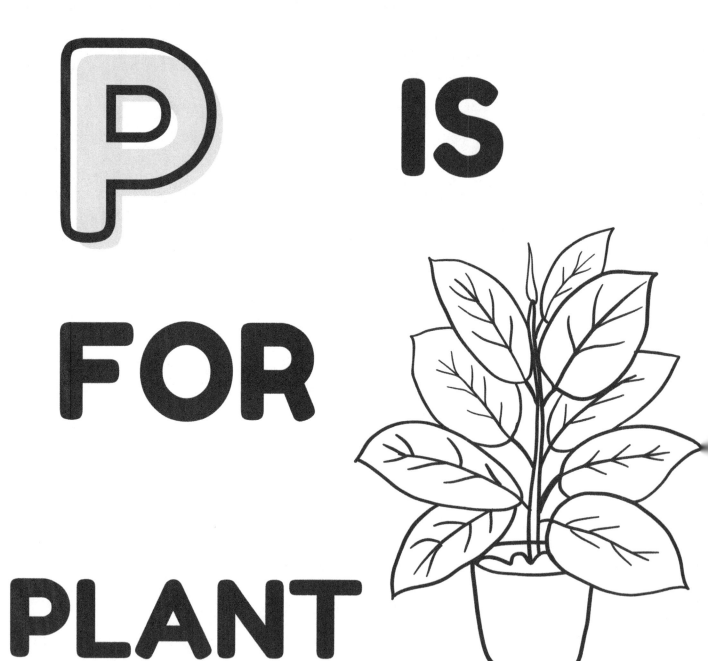

I SPY WITH MY LITTLE EYE SOMETHING BEGINNING WITH...

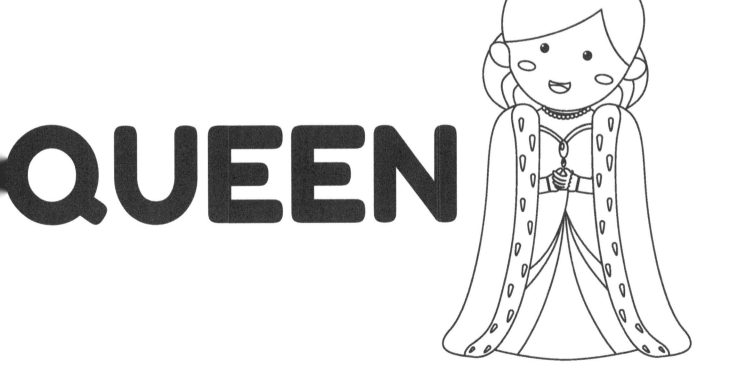

I SPY WITH MY LITTLE EYE SOMETHING BEGINNING WITH...

 R IS FOR

ROOSTER

I SPY WITH MY LITTLE EYE
SOMETHING BEGINNING WITH...

S IS FOR SHEEP

I SPY WITH MY LITTLE EYE SOMETHING BEGINNING WITH...

T IS FOR

TULIP

I SPY WITH MY LITTLE EYE SOMETHING BEGINNING WITH...

U IS FOR

UMBRELLA

I SPY WITH MY LITTLE EYE SOMETHING BEGINNING WITH...

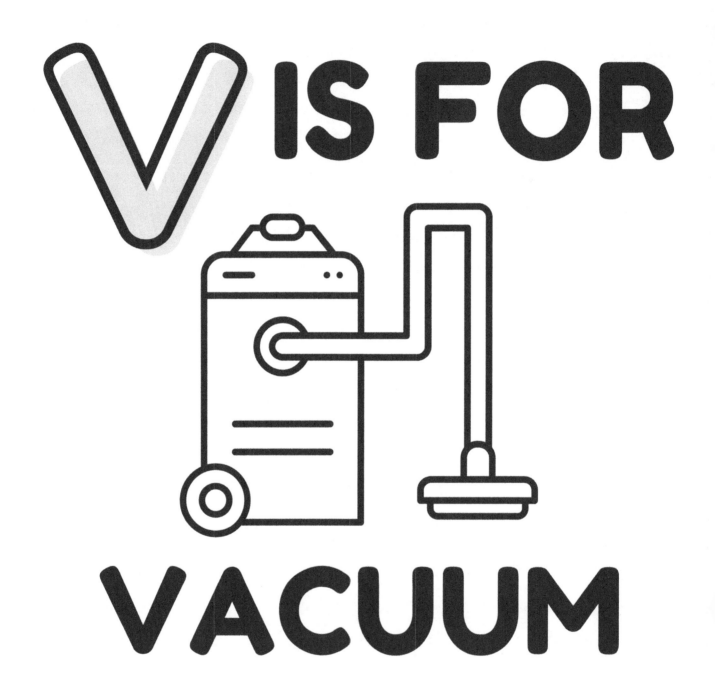

V IS FOR

VACUUM

I SPY WITH MY LITTLE EYE SOMETHING BEGINNING WITH...

W IS

FOR

WATERMELON

I SPY WITH MY LITTLE EYE SOMETHING BEGINNING WITH...

IS FOR

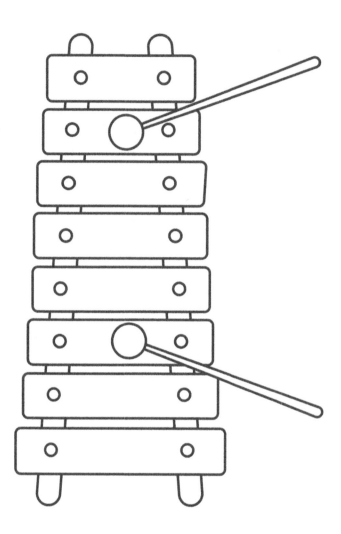

XYLOPHONE

I SPY WITH MY LITTLE EYE SOMETHING BEGINNING WITH...

Y IS FOR

YOUGURT

I SPY WITH MY LITTLE EYE SOMETHING BEGINNING WITH...

Z IS FOR

ZEBRA

I SPY AND COUNT

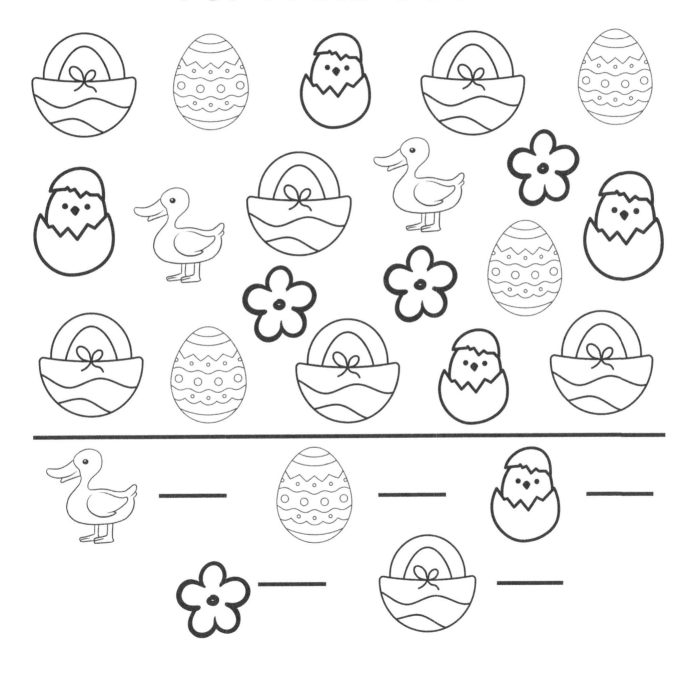

I SPY AND COUNT

I SPY AND COUNT

I SPY AND COUNT

I SPY AND COUNT

I SPY AND COUNT

I SPY AND COUNT

I SPY AND COUNT

I SPY AND COUNT

Made in the USA
Las Vegas, NV
18 March 2024